INFINITY MIRROR

BY ROGER HURN

ILLUSTRATED BY
ALEKSANDAR SOTIROVSKI

9 397002

Titles in the Full Flight Adventure series:

Planet Talent	David Orme
Invaders	Danny Pearson
Alien Exchange	Melanie Joyce
Camp Terror	Craig Allen
White Water	Jane A C West
Infinity Mirror	Roger Hurn
Robot Rampage	Jillian Powell
Stone End Stadium	Richard Taylor
Weed Killers	Jonny Zucker
Dynamite Deputy	Barbara Catchpole

Badger Publishing Limited
Suite G08, Stevenage,
Hertfordshire SG1 2DX
Telephone: 01438 791037 Fax: 01438 791036
www.badgerlearning.co.uk

Infinity Mirror ISBN 978-1-84926-571-3

Publisher: Susan Ross
Senior Editor: Danny Pearson
Series Editor: Jonny Zucker
Designer: Fiona Grant
Illustrator: Aleksandar Sotirovski

Infinity Mirror

Contents

New words:

poltergeist

parallel universe

infinity

reverses

disappear

exist

mysterious

midnight

Main characters:

Chapter 1

Ghosts

Amy's family had just moved into an old spooky house. This didn't scare Amy. She thought it was cool.

She loved ghost stories. Her favourite book was 'Horrible Hauntings'.

"Hey, Mum," she asked, "is this house haunted?"

"No, it isn't," laughed her Mum. "Ghosts aren't real."

Amy frowned. "Well, in my book it says they are."

Amy's Dad looked cross. "There are no such things as ghosts," he said.

Amy also liked playing tricks on people.

She LOVED playing tricks on her younger brother Jed.

That night Jed sneaked out of bed.

He tiptoed into the kitchen and raided the fridge for a midnight snack.

He took a big bite out of a slab of cheese. It tasted awful.

“Yuk!” he shrieked.

He tried to spit it out and bubbles came floating out of his mouth.

Someone has swapped the cheese for a bar of yellow soap!

It must have been Amy, thought Jed angrily.

Suddenly the kitchen light went on. Mum and Dad were standing there in their pyjamas.

Amy came running up behind them.

"What's going on?" asked Dad.

"Amy put a bar of soap in the fridge," said Jed, bursting into tears. "She's trying to poison me!"

"No, I didn't!" said Amy angrily.

"If you didn't do it, who did?" asked Dad.

"Maybe it was a ghost," shrugged Amy.

Mum, Dad and Jed all stared at Amy.

"Don't be silly," said Dad. "We've told you ghosts do not exist!"

"That's right," said Mum. "No more ghosts and no more practical jokes Amy, or you will be in big trouble!"

Chapter 2

Grounded!

The next morning Mum came into Amy's room. Amy was reading 'Horrible Hauntings'.

"Put your book down, Amy," said Mum firmly. "I want you to help me clean your room."

Amy pulled a face. "Do I have to?" she groaned. "I have just got to the bit about poltergeists. Do you know that they..."

"Please Amy!" snapped Mum. "I don't want to hear about ghost stories. We have got work to do. Now plug in the vacuum cleaner."

Amy did as she was told. Mum switched it on but instead of sucking up dirt the vacuum cleaner blew it all over Mum.

Mum was furious. “You heard what we said Amy! No more stupid jokes!”

“It wasn’t me!” shouted Amy.

Mum ignored her and stormed out of the room.

Amy went into the living room.

Dad was waving the remote control at the TV. “I don’t know what’s going on,” he said crossly. “I’m trying to watch the football but the channel keeps switching to a boring cookery show!”

He turned to glare at Amy. “Have you been messing about with the TV?” he asked. “Is this another of your jokes?”

“No!” replied Amy.

Then Mum came in with Jed. “Amy fixed the vacuum cleaner so I got covered in dust,” said Mum.

“And she made me eat soap,” said Jed.

Dad looked puzzled. “Why are you doing this, Amy?” he asked.

“I’m not,” said Amy. “But I think I know who is.”

Mum, Dad and Jed all looked at Amy.

“Well?” said Dad

“In my ‘Horrible Hauntings’ book it says that poltergeists play practical jokes when they haunt a house. I think our house is haunted by a poltergeist!”

“That’s it!” snapped Mum, “you’re grounded!”

Chapter 3

The Poltergeist

Amy was upset. Everyone was cross with her. They didn't believe her when she said the house was haunted.

Dad even took her 'Horrible Hauntings' book away.

"We mean it Amy," said Mum. "No more stupid talk about ghosts and haunting and no more practical jokes!"

Amy was sitting, sulking on her bed when her mobile phone began to buzz.

Someone had sent her a text. Amy read the mysterious message.

TURN ON THE TV AND SWITCH TO CHANNEL 999.

She did so, but the picture was fuzzy and white dots filled the screen like a snowstorm.

“Huh?” said Amy. “This is rubbish.”

She went to switch the TV off but it stayed on and the dots started to move together. Amy stared at the TV.

She moved closer to take a better look.

Suddenly a face appeared on the screen.

Amy squealed in terror. It was not a human face... it was the face of a poltergeist!

Chapter 4

Trapped

The poltergeist's face loomed forward and filled the screen.

Its eyes were like two chips of black ice. It pointed at Amy.

Amy stumbled backwards. Her heart was pounding.

She tried to scream but no sound came out of her bone dry mouth.

Then the poltergeist spoke. “Don’t be afraid,” it said. “I won’t harm you.”

Amy gulped down her fear. The ghost sounded sad, not evil.

Then she remembered the tricks. “Was it you who put the soap in the fridge?”

The ghost nodded sadly. “I also did the vacuum cleaner and the TV remote,” it said.

“Why?” asked Amy.

“Because I needed to grab your attention.”

"OK, you've got it now," replied Amy.

Then she smiled. "Hey, I told Mum and Dad our house was haunted by a poltergeist and I was right!"

"But I'm not a poltergeist," replied the creature. "My name is Zeta and I'm an alien from a parallel universe."

Amy's eyebrows shot up her forehead in surprise. "So what are you doing in my TV?" she said.

Zeta explained that she had travelled to Earth by using an 'Infinity Mirror'.

"You can use it to step into different worlds," she said. "But it has a strange effect."

"What's that?" asked Amy.

"It reverses everything," replied Zeta. "So, in your world I look like a ghost – even though I'm not."

Amy blinked hard. "So are all ghosts really just aliens like you?"

"Yes," nodded Zeta. "We like to go on holiday to different worlds and Earth is a very popular place to visit. But I broke my Infinity Mirror when I arrived and now I'm stuck here."

Amy frowned. "Hey, it's seven years bad luck if you break a mirror," she said.

"It's much worse than that," sighed Zeta. "If you can't help me find a way to return home I'm doomed to stay here on Earth, not just for seven years but forever!"

Chapter 5

Home Time

Amy frowned. “Don’t worry, Zeta,” she said. “I’ll think of something.”

Amy scratched her head. She paced up and down her bedroom. Then she sat down on her bed. “It’s no good,” she said. “I don’t have a clue how to help you.”

Zeta groaned. “I don’t want to be a ghost,” she said. “I don’t want to spend my life haunting houses. I want to go home.”

“Wait a minute,” said Amy, clicking her fingers. “You’ve just given me an idea.”

She ran to find her ‘Horrible Hauntings’ book. “This book has a chapter called ‘How to Stop Ghosts Haunting Your House’,” she said.

She opened it. “Ah, here is the page,” she exclaimed, “and it’s also about mirrors.”

“Go on,” said Zeta.

"It says that one way to make ghosts vanish is to put two mirrors facing each other. Then, when the ghost floats between the mirrors it will disappear."

Zeta looked terrified. "But what if it doesn't work? What if I just disappear?"

Amy gulped. "I don't know, but it's our only hope."

Just then they heard Mum call from downstairs.

"Oh no," gasped Amy. "That's Mum coming to check up on me. Come on, Zeta, there's no time to lose!"

Amy grabbed two mirrors and set them up. There was a popping sound as Zeta flew out of the TV and into the room.

Mum's footsteps sounded on the stairs.

"Hurry!" hissed Amy.

"No," said Zeta, "I'm too scared."

"You must," said Amy. "Trust me. I'm sure it will work."

At that second Mum knocked on the door.

The 'alien' took a big breath and shot between the mirrors.

Her reflections went on for ever.

She started to vanish just as the door opened and Amy's Mum stepped into the room.

Amy's Mum stared at the book in Amy's hand.

"What are you doing with that book, Amy?" she asked. "We said you were not to read any more ghost stories."

"Don't worry, Mum," replied Amy, closing the book. "I know now that ghosts aren't real."

"Really?" said Mum, her face breaking into a smile. "I'm very pleased to hear it; so pleased, in fact, that I'll let you come down and have your tea with us."

Amy grinned back at her. "I'll just put the book away then I'll be there," she said.

Mum nodded and left. Amy spun round and ran to the mirrors.

There was no sign at all of Zeta but Amy heard a very faint ghostly voice saying: "Thank you Amy, it worked! I'm home!"

Interesting Mirror Facts

- *A mirror can be any smooth, shiny surface that reflects or bounces back light.*

- *You can see yourself in a mirror because light rays reflected from your body bounce off the mirror's shiny surface and back into your eyes.*

- *When you look in a mirror you are seeing yourself reflected backwards. This is called a mirror image.*

- *The ancient Greeks and Romans used highly polished metal disks as mirrors.*

- *Modern mirrors are made of glass with a thin coating of metal on the back.*

• *There are three types of mirrors: flat, concave and convex.*

Plane mirrors are flat.

Concave mirrors curve inward.

Convex mirrors curve outward.

• *The wicked Queen in 'Snow White' had a magical mirror.*

• *Infinity mirrors do exist but sadly you can't use them to visit an alien world.*

Joke

Q: What do you call a prehistoric ghost?
A: A terror - dactyl!

Questions about the Story

- *What is Amy's favourite book?*

- *What happens to Jed when he raids the fridge?*

- *Who does Jed blame?*

- *What happens when Mum switches on the vacuum cleaner?*

- *What happens when Dad tries to watch the big match on TV?*

- *Which TV channel does Amy turn on?*

- *Who is Zeta?*

- *What does Zeta use to travel to our world?*

- *What does Amy use to send Zeta home?*

- *Why does Mum let Amy come down for tea?*